Contents

COLOUR FIRST READER books are perfect for
beginner readers. All the text inside this Colour First
Reader book has been checked and approved by a
reading specialist, so it is the ideal size, length
and level for children learning to read.

Series Reading Consultant: Prue Goodwin
Honorary Fellow of the University of Reading

Chapter One

High in the spooky mountains, a spooky storm was raging. In the heart of that spooky storm, there stood a spooky old castle. In that spooky old castle, there was a spooky laboratory. And in that spooky laboratory ...

Something very, very *spooky* was going on.

Vast vats were hubbling and
bubbling. Enormous machines
were humming and thrumming.
Colossal coils were whizzing
and fizzing. And right in the
middle of all that sound and
fury was . . . The Doctor.

He pulled a massive lever.

The roof opened
wide to the night,
and the wild wind
came whistling in.
Thunder crashed,
lightning flashed . . .
and *ZAPPED!* on
to a metal rod. It
sizzled down the
wall, scorched across the
floor, and jumped
once more . . .

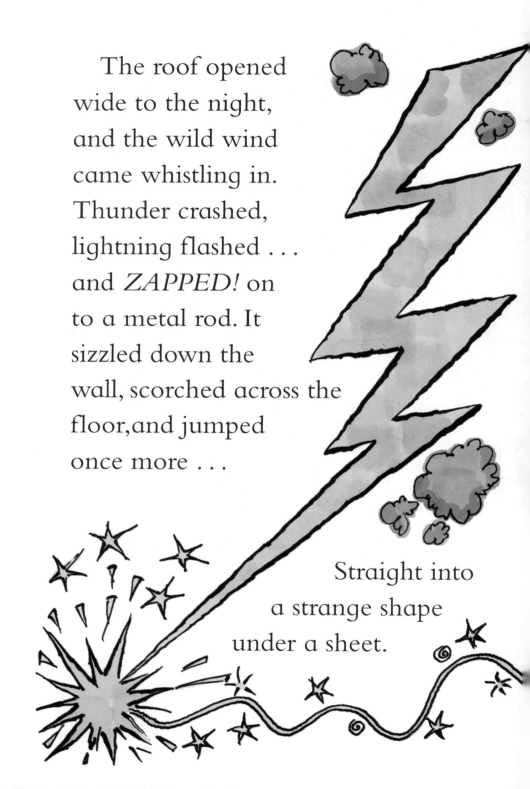

Straight into
a strange shape
under a sheet.

The Doctor threw some switches. Bright sparks flew, choking smoke billowed, and The Doctor checked his dials. He looked around – and then he smiled. Beneath the sheet there were definitely some ... twitches.

11

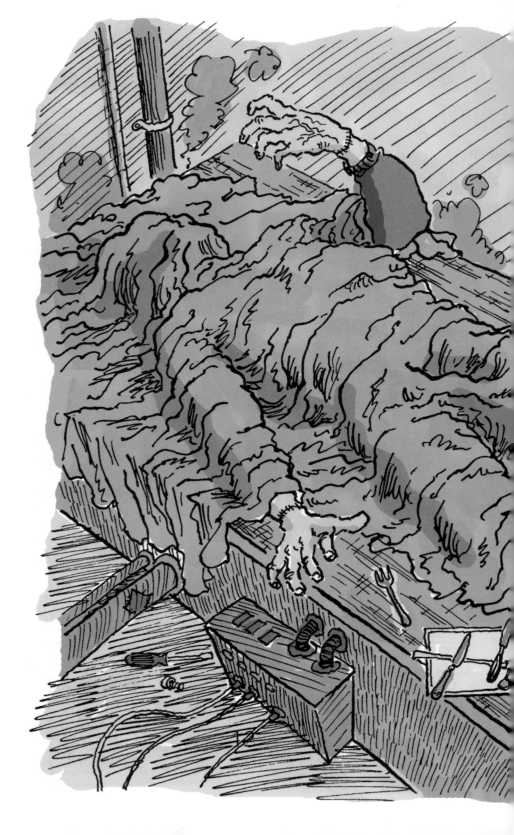

Suddenly, the shape sat up and the sheet fell away. A hideous creature was revealed. The creature rose to its giant feet. It stamped stiffly towards The Doctor.

It reached out
with its giant
hands. It moaned
and it groaned.

Outside the storm
was passing and the
wind dying down.

"I . . . want . . .
to . . . be . . ." the
creature growled.
"A . . . teacher."

"Are you sure about that?"
said The Doctor, a bit surprised.

"Absolutely," said the creature,
its eyes gleaming.

"Well, it's your funeral," said
The Doctor, and shrugged. He
turned the machines off and
put the kettle on.

17

So The Doctor got the creature into Teacher Training College. The creature worked hard, and one day he wasn't just a creature any more. He had a posh piece of paper that said he was . . .

Now all he needed was a class to teach . . .

Chapter Two

Down at the foot of the spooky mountains, there was a little town. At the edge of that little town, there stood a little school. At the heart of that little school, there was a little classroom. And in that little classroom . . .

19

Something very, very *little* had escaped.

Most of the children were laughing and cheering. A few of them were screaming and squealing. Two of them were chasing and leaping.

And right in the middle of all
that sound and fury was . . .
Mrs Shelley, the head.

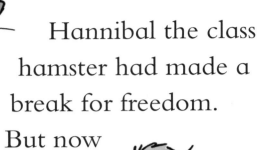

Hannibal the class
hamster had made a
break for freedom.
But now
he was almost
trapped. He
ducked and
dived, he weaved
and bobbed, he scampered
this way and that across the
floor, then jumped
once more . . .

Straight into the cage from where he'd started.

"Thank goodness for that," said Mrs Shelley, shutting the cage door with a *PING!* "I'd better speak to your new teacher about Hannibal," she said. "I don't want him causing as much chaos in the school as he did last term."

"Who is our new teacher, Miss?" asked one of the children.

"You'll soon find out," said Mrs Shelley. "Ah, I think I hear him now."

The children listened. There was a *THUD!* outside in the corridor. Then another, and another . . .

Somebody was heading
steadily towards their classroom.
Somebody with *very* heavy feet, it
seemed.

The floor shook. The tables
and chairs shook. The *children*
shook.

Suddenly, the door creaked
open . . . and a huge figure
loomed over them. It was . . .

...the FRANKENSTEIN teacher!

The class gasped, and shook
even more. Hannibal squeaked,
and fell off his exercise wheel.

"Pay attention please,
everybody," said Mrs Shelley.
"This is your new teacher, Mr
Frankenstein, which
makes you class 3F, of
course. Now, what do
we say, Class 3F? We
say, *Good morning,
Mr Frankenstein.*"

Mrs Shelley waited. But Class 3F just sat there, shaking and silent.

"Come along, children," said Mrs Shelley. "Where are your manners?"

Class 3F didn't say a word. They were totally stunned.

"That's not a very nice welcome, Class 3F," said Mrs Shelley crossly. "I hope you're just shy today. Well, I'll leave them in your capable hands, Mr Frankenstein," she said, turning to leave. "I'm sure everything will be fine."

Mrs Shelley couldn't have been more wrong if she'd tried.

Chapter Three

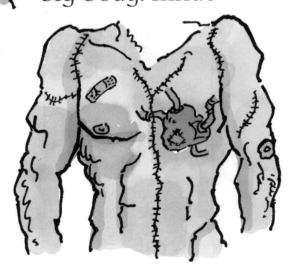

At the front of the little classroom, there stood The Frankenstein Teacher in his big suit. Inside that big suit, there was his big body. Inside that big body, there beat his big heart. And inside

that big heart . . .

Something very,
very . . . *big* was
being felt.

After all, this was the
biggest day of The Frankenstein
Teacher's life. Unlike The Doctor,
The Frankenstein Teacher *loved*
kids. He couldn't think of a
better job than being a teacher.
He was desperate to do it well.

He was desperate for the kids to like him, too.

The children of Class 3F were starting to relax, at least. Most of them were staring at The Frankenstein Teacher. But a few of them were whispering to each other. And two of them actually put their hands up.

"Er . . . yes?" said The Frankenstein Teacher, in

his growly voice. He pointed
at the nearest child who wanted
to ask a question.

"Why are you
so . . . ugly, Sir?"
said the child, a
cheeky boy. The
class exploded
into sniggers and
giggles, and relaxed
a whole lot more.

"Excuse me?" said The Frankenstein Teacher, a bit surprised.

"Please, Sir!" called out the second child with a hand up.

"Yes?" said The Frankenstein Teacher, turning to her.

"Hannibal's escaped again, Sir!" she said, and the same old panic began.

34

Pretty soon most of the
children were laughing and
cheering, a few of them were
screaming and squealing, and
two of them were chasing and
leaping. And right in the middle
of all that sound and fury was . . .

The not-so-happy
Frankenstein Teacher, doing
his best.

He helped catch Hannibal.
He stamped stiffly round the
classroom with his giant feet,

He reached out with his
giant hands. He held on to the
hamster . . . and gently eased
him back in his cage.

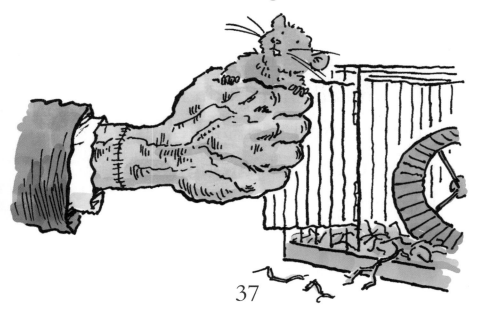

But that word *ugly* kept ringing through his brain.

He noticed the children kept out of his way, although they hung around the other teachers. He noticed the children had plenty to say, although only when they thought he wasn't listening.

And by the end of the day . . .

The Frankenstein Teacher was
very . . . depressed.

"They don't like me, Hannibal," he said sadly to the only friend he'd made. "It's because of how I look, isn't it?"

Hannibal peeked in his mirror too, and squeaked.

"Though I suppose I could change that, couldn't I . . . ?"

Chapter Four

On the opposite edge of the
little town from the school, there
stood a shiny new shopping mall.
In the heart of that shiny new
shopping mall, there was a shiny
new clothes shop. And in that
shiny new clothes shop . . .

Something very, very . . . *shiny
and new* was being tried on.

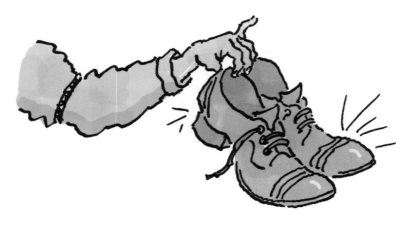

So The Frankenstein Teacher
bought the shiny new suit, and
loads of other stuff. He had his
hair cut in a smart style, and his
nails trimmed, and he worked
hard at his smile. Soon he felt
much more . . . sure of himself.

Now all he needed was a
certain class's approval . . .

The next morning, the
classroom filled up as usual.
Class 3F sat and waited for
their teacher . . . and
waited . . . and waited.

The children listened.

Somebody was heading steadily towards the classroom. Someone who still had very heavy feet.

The floor shook. The tables and chairs shook. The *children* shook.

Suddenly the door creaked open . . . and a huge figure stood framed in the light. It was The Frankenstein Teacher, grinning for all he was worth.

The class gasped, and shook
even more . . . only with *laughter*
this time.

Hannibal squeaked and fell off his exercise wheel again. But nobody noticed. Class 3F was too busy laughing at the person in front of them.

"Er . . . OK, Class 3F," he growled at last, still smiling. "What's the joke?"

"You are, Sir," a boy spluttered, and the class howled, until the whole school could hear them. The Frankenstein Teacher didn't say a word.

But the smile slowly faded from his face.

Chapter Five

Across the gloomy sky, some gloomy clouds were gathering. Beneath those gloomy clouds, there stood a gloomy school. In that gloomy school, there was a gloomy head's office. And in that gloomy head's office . . .

Something very, very . . . *gloomy* was happening.

After all, this was the gloomiest
moment of The Frankenstein
Teacher's life. He'd tried to do
a good job. He'd done his best
to make the children like him.
But their laughter kept ringing
through his brain.

So he had decided to give up
being a teacher.

"Are you sure about that?" said Mrs Shelley, a bit surprised. The Frankenstein Teacher nodded gloomily. "Oh, well," said Mrs Shelley, rather sadly. "I hope you'll stay with us for the rest of the day, at least."

The Frankenstein Teacher trudged back to the classroom with Mrs Shelley,

Mrs Shelley told Class 3F the news.

Well, Class 3F I hope you aren't to blame for the school losing such a highly qualified teacher as Mr Frankenstein. Teachers like him don't grow on trees, you know. They're extremely hard to find.

But Class 3F weren't impressed. In fact, they couldn't see what the fuss was about. How could somebody so *ugly* be worth having? They just wanted a new teacher. Any teacher who was better looking.

And who wore nice, sensible teacher clothes.

The clock ticked on, and time slid past, until home time came around at last. Then, with a sigh, The Frankenstein Teacher said goodbye . . . and left.

At the school gates, grown-ups were moaning and groaning. Children were teasing and squeezing. Babies were squalling and bawling. And right in the middle of all that sound and fury was . . . a hamster on the run.

Look, it's Hannibal! He's escaped again!

"Quick, after him!" shouted a boy, and Class 3F gave chase.

But Hannibal kept up a furious pace. He ducked and dived, he weaved and bobbed, he searched this way and that for a pair of heavy feet. And there they were, heading steadily along . . . the other side of the street!

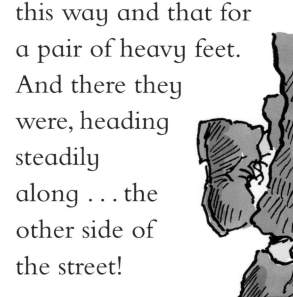

Hannibal paused. The children were closing in on him from behind, and thoughts of road safety fled from his mind. Hannibal rushed out to follow his friend, and then with a . . . *SPLAT!* – he met a swift end.

Mrs Shelley had run him over
with her car.

Chapter Six

It was an accident, of course, and poor Mrs Shelley was very upset. The children were stunned and pale. A few of them had started to wail.

Two of them were saying that somebody should take Hannibal to the vet.

"I think it's too late for that," growled The Frankenstein Teacher.

He stamped swiftly through the crowd of people with his giant feet . . .

THUD! THUD!

He reached out with his giant
hands. He picked up the little
splattered hamster. He held
Hannibal gently in his giant
arms.

A giant tear rolled down his cheek.

And that's when Class 3F saw that there was more to their ex-teacher than met the eye. He might be ugly, but he felt sad enough to cry! So under that hideous surface, he must be a . . . *pretty nice guy.*

Just then, thunder boomed, and
lightning split the sky.

"No," said The Frankenstein
Teacher. "But I know a man who
can."

High in the spooky mountains, a spooky storm was raging. In the heart of that spooky storm, there stood a spooky old castle. In that spooky old castle, there was a spooky laboratory. And in that spooky laboratory . . .

You know *exactly* what kind of spookiness was going on.

There was a hubbling and
bubbling and humming and
thrumming and whizzing
and fizzing and crashing and
flashing and *ZAPPING* and
sizzling and switching and some
twitching . . . in a strange little
shape under a sheet.

"It lives!" The Doctor shouted.
And The Frankenstein Teacher
smiled.

He did a lot more smiling
later. Back at school, Class 3F
were waiting for him. This time
he got a much nicer welcome,
especially when the children saw
that Hannibal was . . . OK! Mrs
Shelley was very relieved.

Hannibal looked a bit different from the way he used to before he was splattered. Though now class 3F realized . . . *how you look doesn't matter.*

"Three cheers for Mr Frankenstein, the best teacher in the world!" somebody yelled.

The Frankenstein Teacher
didn't know what to say.

But he knew in his big heart,
this was truly . . . his happiest
day!

Colour First Readers

Welcome to Colour First Readers. The following pages are intended for any adults (parents, relatives, teachers) who may buy these books to share the stories with youngsters. The pages explain a little about the different stages of learning to read and offer some suggestions about how best to support children at a very important point in their reading development.

Children start to learn about reading as soon someone reads a book aloud to them when they are babies. Book-loving babies grow into toddlers who enjoy sitting on a lap listening to a story, looking at pictures or joining in with familiar words. Young children who have listened to stories start school with an expectation of enjoyment from books and this positive outlook helps as they are taught to read in the more formal context of school.

Cracking the code

Before they can enjoy reading for and to themselves, all children have to learn how to crack the alphabetic code and make meaning out of the lines and squiggles we call letters and punctuation. Some lucky pupils find the process of learning to read undemanding; some find it very hard.

Most children, within two or three years, become confident at working out what is written on the page. During this time they will probably read collections of books which are graded; that is, the books introduce a few new words and increase in length, thus helping youngsters gradually to build up their growing ability to work out the words and understand basic meanings.

Eventually, children will reach a crucial point when, without any extra help, they can decode words in an entire book, albeit a short one. They then enter the next phase of becoming a reader.

Making meaning

It is essential, at this point, that children stop seeing progress as gradually 'climbing a ladder' of books of ever-increasing difficulty. There is a transition stage between building word recognition skills and enjoying reading a story. Up until now, success has depended on getting the words right but to get pleasure from reading to themselves, children need to fully comprehend the content of what they read. Comprehension will only be reached if focus is put on understanding meaning and that can only happen if the reader is not hesitant when decoding. At this fragile, transition stage, decoding should be so easy that it slowly becomes automatic. Reading a book with ease enables children to get lost in the story, to enjoy the unfolding narrative at the same time as perfecting their newly learned word recognition skills.

At this stage in their reading development, children need to:

- Practice their newly established early decoding skills at a level which eventually enables them to do it automatically

- Concentrate on making sensible meanings from the words they decode

- Develop their ability to understand when meanings are 'between the lines' and other use of literary language

- Be introduced, very gradually, to longer books in order to build up stamina as readers

In other words, new readers need books that are well within their reading ability and that offer easy encounters with humour, inference, plot-twists etc. In the past, there have been very few children's books that provided children with these vital experiences at an early stage. Indeed, some children had to leap from highly controlled teaching materials to junior novels.

This experience often led to reluctance in youngsters who were not yet confident enough to tackle longer books.

Matching the books to reading development

Colour First Readers fill the gap between early reading and children's literature and, in doing so, support inexperienced readers at a vital time in their reading development. Reading aloud to children continues to be very important even after children have learned to read and, as they are well written by popular children's authors, Colour First Readers are great to read aloud. The stories provide plenty of opportunities for adults to demonstrate different voices or expression and, in a short time, give lots to talk about and enjoy together.

Each book in the series combines a number of highly beneficial features, including:

- Well-written and enjoyable stories by popular children's authors

- Unthreatening amounts of print on a page

- Unrestricted but accessible vocabularies

- A wide interest age to suit the different ages at which children might reach the transition stage of reading development

- Different sorts of stories – traditional, set in the past, present or future, real life and fantasy, comic and serious, adventures, mysteries etc.

- A range of engaging illustrations by different illustrators

- Stories which are as good to read aloud to children as they are to be read alone

All in all, Colour First Readers are to be welcomed for children throughout the early primary school years – not only for learning to read but also as a series of good stories to be shared by everyone.
I like to think that the word 'Readers' in the title of this series refers to the many young children who will enjoy these books on their journey to becoming lifelong bookworms.

Prue Goodwin
Honorary Fellow of the University of Reading

Helping children to enjoy *The Frankenstein Teacher*

If a child can read a page or two fluently, without struggling with the words at all, then he/she should be able to read this book alone. However, children are all different and need different levels of support to help them become confident enough to read a book to themselves.

Some young readers will not need any help to get going; they can just get on with enjoying the story. Others may lack confidence and need help getting into the story. For these children, it may help if you talk about what might happen in the book.

Explore the title, cover and first few illustrations with them, making comments and suggestions about any clues to what might happen in the story. Read the first chapter aloud together. Don't make it a chore. If they are still reluctant to do it alone, read the whole book with them, making it an enjoyable experience.

The following suggestions will not be necessary every time a book is read but, every so often, when a story has been particularly enjoyed, children love responding to it through creative activities.

Before reading

Dr Frankenstein and his Creature are icons of English literature and this book depends on some knowledge of the original tale. Most people will know the characters' names and have some idea of the plot. Even very young children may have seen TV shows or comics that featured Frankenstein but they may not know the details of the tale. Creating the 'monster' is an important element of *The Frankenstein Teacher* so read Chapter One together to introduce the idea.

During reading

Asking questions about a story can be really helpful to support understanding but don't ask too many – and don't make it into a test on what happens. Relate the questions to the child's own experiences and imagination.

In Chapter Two, for example, ask: 'Is this school like yours?'; or 'How would you feel if a Frankenstein Teacher walked in to your class?'

Responding to the book

If your child has enjoyed the story, it can increase the fun to do something creative in response. If possible, provide art materials and dressing-up clothes so that they can make things, play at being characters, write and draw, act out a scene or respond in some other way to the story.

Activities for children

If you have enjoyed reading this story, you could:

- Make a Frankenstein mask and terrify your family.

- Share the story with your friends and make up a play to show the rest of your class

- Get a piece of paper and a pen to do the Frankenstein Quiz:

  1. **Who wrote** *The Frankenstein Teacher*?

  2. **At the beginning, how does The Doctor bring his creation to life?**

  3. **Where does the creature go to learn to be a teacher?**

  4. **In the little school, what is the head teacher's name?**

  5. **Who is called Hannibal?**

  6. **What does The Doctor do to Hannibal?**

- Write your own story about what happens next to the Frankenstein Teacher. Look at how the author uses words – lots of rhymes ("whizzing and fizzing"), repetition of sounds ("wild wind came whistling") and of words ("spooky" in Chapter One and "little" in Chapter Two). Try to write your story in the same way.

ALSO AVAILABLE AS COLOUR FIRST READERS